WANTED FOR LOVE

Roger Osborne

Wanted for Love

A dating success story of a man over 40

Copyright © 2022 Roger Osborne

Cover image designed by Freepik.

Table of Contents

The goal...4

The opportunity...7

22 July..10

1 August..12

2 August..14

4 August..17

7 August..21

13, 14, 15, 16, 17, 18, 19, 20 August.............................23

21 August...25

24 August...27

29 August...29

4 September..31

The meeting..33

The goal

"Dear Roger, I received your email, and I must say that you are pretty messed up in life too! Because of work, home, and children, you don't have any time left for yourself. So I believe you need to wait a little longer before you can think about starting to build a relationship with someone. Don't feel bad, but I think it's not the right time to start something. Sorry. Greetings, Kate."

The email was simple, direct, but lapidary. Kate was right.

I had been trying for two years to meet a woman who could become my partner. I had tried everything, almost systematically, as it is in my character to do so when faced with a severe problem. The great need I felt for a companion pushed me to consider every possible way of contact. I looked to all of my personal contacts, even in the work environment, and hung out with friends with several possible contacts. But, so far, nothing at all.

I attempted to answer marriage announcements, and I quickly discovered that they can be classified into two categories: marriage agencies and prostitutes. There was a moment when I was tempted to use an agency. One day, I received a phone call from a marriage agency about my text message for an ad. The woman was so friendly that I let myself be convinced to go and see her. During the interview, she was very professional and kind, not to mention helpful. I thought it could work, but unfortunately, the insurmountable obstacle was the cost. I couldn't afford it, and then, at the end of the day, I always had the doubt that their goal was to get me to the end of the term, regardless of the result, leaving me high and dry.

I changed my strategy and switched to Internet ads. Again, I found a lot of prostitutes, but every now and then, there were some real ads. Though whenever this happens, they turn out to be difficult situations with almost nonexistent chances of success. I told myself, however, that it was worth continuing to try. So I continued to follow the ads assiduously, responding from time to time to those that seemed more legitimate. Once, I was in touch with a woman in my city, and we met up, but then she told me it couldn't work. Probably I simply was not her ideal man.

Another way I experimented was with so-called dating sites. There are a lot of websites that specialize in dating, and each site is more or less professional. In this case, the experience was quite varied. Almost all websites invite you to sign up for free, allow you to search for people with various criteria, and allow for more or less complete viewing of the cards. Nearly all ask for a subscription to see all the data and correspond, even by email. These elements limit the possibilities because, until communication with the person is established, it is impossible to know if a relationship will work, even if only as a friendship.

Another aspect of dating sites is the type of people who frequent them. Being a man, I can only talk about the women I encountered. Apart from the usual prostitutes, there are many girls or married women interested in simple correspondence, many homosexuals, and many looking for the impossible man. The percentage of regular women looking for ordinary men is negligible. Hence, once again, there is a very low probability of finding an interesting person on these sites. However, I decided to continue to follow this path, like the ads, because it did not cost me anything to check the Internet from time to time.

The opportunity

When I found the website, I was puzzled, as I didn't think there could be a completely free dating site. But there it was. This site would let you view complete cards, photos, and even large versions of photos. But the most significant thing: it would allow you to communicate with the person. All without having to make any subscriptions.

I thought: "Great!" This could be my chance to contact a much larger number of people than I had been able to find so far. I was pleasantly surprised to learn that the site was frequented by many women looking for partners. Also, the site had effective control measures against both prostitutes and scammers.

Yes, scammers. Unfortunately, the Internet is full of characters who try to lure people by leveraging basic needs, such as love or economic ones, only to rob them. Fortunately, I have always been critical of strangers. Furthermore, my previous work history allowed me to identify the deceptive nature of these scammers quickly. Once, they managed to take me almost to the end of the process, but I unmasked them and, fortunately, didn't lose anything.

Excited that I had found a new opportunity, I immediately began searching through the people on the site. I knew that I would have to contact several people and that almost all of them would be unsuitable, so I organized myself in a particular way. Once I selected someone, based on the first impression received from their photo, I went to examine the card to verify age, physical characteristics, aspirations and the type of man they were looking for. If there were enough compatibilities, I contacted them and waited.

Obviously, only a few women responded, but luckily the archive contained a very high number of people. I have to say that almost all the people I managed to contact had one big flaw. They were elusive, indecisive, and unreliable, and they didn't answer my questions. I deduced that they were obviously not really interested in forming a relationship..

Later I discovered that many of these sites fill their archives with fake profiles, and the chats of these fake profiles are professionally managed. Basically, you are talking to an employee whose only job is to entertain you. Often these sites prevent you from sending personal contact information through chat messages, making it impossible to actually get to know a person. But what's the point? The most honest ones declare in their Terms of Service that the website's purpose is to entertain people, not help them meet, and that the site is full of fake profiles.

I knew this was going to be tough, but after months and months of trying, I was beginning to despair. Maybe Kate was right. I had to make my peace with it; wait for the kids to grow up, wait until I had a lot more time for myself, and then start searching again.

Yes, wait, but for how long? I was approaching 50, and it seemed that the more time passed, the more my chances faded. I tried to think about the kind of women who might be interested in me. A young girl might have come to me just for money, and I didn't have any; a lady, let's say well-off, would have had other opportunities to find a companion. That left the regular women who were divorced or single and about my age. Do you know a single or divorced forty-year-old woman?

But this opens another big question. A woman of this type, nowadays, is definitely a mature woman who knows what she wants, especially what she does not want to lose. Living together is very difficult unless one of the two imposes himself on the other, and that's not good. That's why I began to wonder whether it might be possible to find a forty-year-old woman who was single or divorced but, coming from a different culture, had a softer attitude.

Not that I'm a male chauvinist. Quite the contrary. I respect women and believe that men and women are the same. In a partnership, the two are on the same level, with no one overpowering the other. I agree that we need to share tasks and help each other with household chores, such as washing dishes, laundry, etc. But, the sharing must be mutual and ongoing. Alternatively, you can agree beforehand to split up the tasks. While I tend to have old-fashioned attitude, I don't shy away from mutual cooperation and doing chores at home.

22 July

Today I came in contact with a woman who seems different from the others. I approached her yesterday after seeing her photos and card; she looked interesting to me. Her name is Yulia. She is my age, is looking for a life partner, and seems quite in line with what I am looking for in regards to aesthetics and character and aspirations.

Today I managed to have a few words with her, finding her intriguing because, unlike the other experiences I've had so far, we talk fluidly. She doesn't talk around subjects and responds directly. In short, she actively participates in the discourse and is easy-going.

Yulia immediately made it clear that she is not interested in cybersex but only in a serious relationship. I answered frankly and without considering whether my response could jeopardize the burgeoning connection. I told her that I like sex a lot, but only together with love, and I am also interested in a serious relationship. Unexpectedly, Yulia gave me her email address, asking me for photos. I haven't put them in my profile for fear of I don't know what. I continue on the path of total sincerity and send her a few recent photos of myself, trembling at the idea of her not liking me, but instead...

"Hi, Roger. I received your email and photos. Thank you! You are a very handsome man." I was stunned, not so much by the fact that she might like me—I knew I'm not that bad—but by how things were unfolding. Within a few hours, I had managed to establish effective communication with a woman simply by making sincerity my top priority. And the amazing thing is the helpfulness, sympathy, and apparent sincerity on Yulia's part.

#

Two years ago, when I started my new life-changing job in a new city with new friends, I told myself that I would be sincere at all costs from then on. I have never liked confrontation, and I have always tried to be accommodating in order to avoid conflict. So when it was necessary to give in, I sacrificed myself and gave in; if it was unavoidable, I even lied. But I learned the hard way that the truth is best, even when it hurts, really hurts. That's why I decided to be honest at all costs. And I must say that it seems that my sincerity in proposing to Yulia paid off. Unbelievably, my frankness was appreciated, and I certainly valued Yulia's. Of course, to be in tune, it takes two people.

1 August

I needed to check out the main issues right away, starting with the most easily identifiable ones—the physical ones. I immediately brought up the subject. I asked if she likes polished nails, heels, and all of the aspects that convey femininity in a woman and that I love so much. The answer was positive. Every time she confirmed my desires, I felt a blow to my heart.

"Is it possible?" I asked myself. Slowly, doubt began to creep in that she was playing dirty. Was she trying to guess, from my questions or from my speeches, what my tastes are and then respond appropriately to meet my expectations?

At a certain point, I asked her how she was dressed. Her answer was sharp and decisive. "I don't like to talk about that." In reality, she was afraid that I would take the conversation toward cybersex, but I didn't know that. I simply noted her answer and changed the subject.

She told me that soon she would go to another city to spend a week on vacation with her girlfriend. I couldn't address it right away, but the information caught my attention. Could she be homosexual? But what is the point of looking for a partner on a dating site? I didn't understand. I went to sleep, determined to clear the matter up at the next meeting.

#

Anyway, I was happy to have found a woman who was feminine. My ideal woman expresses her femininity, her essence. I am not attracted to women who, for example, dress androgynously or, worse, as tomboys. From my point of view, a woman wears skirts and heels, polishes her nails, adorns herself with jewels, wears her hair long, and, yes, must have breasts. In short, the classic image of a woman. This is not to say that a woman can never break out of these canons. This also has to do with eroticism. A woman who expresses her nature, in my opinion, is also erotic in the eyes of a man. And I love eroticism. I don't see anything erotic in a girl wearing sneakers, jeans, or a sweatshirt. Obviously, these are my personal tastes, and I don't consider them universal canons.

2 August

After the customary greetings, I immediately started straight on the question that had been gnawing at me since the night before.

"What do you mean by girlfriend?" The misunderstanding was cleared up immediately. She wasn't a girlfriend but a simple friend. It was just a translation error between Yulia's language and English. Yulia was pretty good at English, but only at reading it. Writing it was a different story, so she had to rely on an online translator, which sometimes made mistakes. It's surprising how many words don't have a corresponding word in other languages. From time to time, I used the translator to understand some of the words she used or translate ones I used. Having clarified the matter, I decided to give her some space since we had not talked about me so far, and I wanted her to get to know me as well, thus putting me to the test. But to my proposal to provide information about myself, she replied: "What kind of woman are you looking for?"

She turned the tables on me! So it's up to me again to say what I'm looking for. I sent her an email with a short, concise, and sincere description of my expectations. Yulia replied that she "liked my letter very much." What? That was not possible! I asked her to confirm, and she said that she agrees with what I'm looking for and corresponds with my wishes. Also, she sent me an email with her wishes. I read it all in one breath and ...

"Yulia, you can't imagine how happy I am!"

I responded, and for the first time, I sent her a virtual kiss (emoticon).

"I'm happy too!" she responded with a virtual kiss.

We agreed that we have the same goals and, on the wave of emotion, I wanted to hear her voice, so I asked for her cell phone number and tried to send her a text message. But it didn't work. We changed the subject, and I asked her, trying to get her to talk first, what kind of music she likes. Even on musical tastes, we agreed! I told her that I think it's easier to find something we disagree on and asked for permission to call her 'my dear'. She accepted and sent me a kiss.

So I suggested sending her some music files, and her response was "Yeeeeeeeeeeeeeeeeeee." I love such enthusiasm, even more so when it comes from an adult. It means that despite her age, her soul is still young and full of life and drive, like me. Then we talked about food, and she told me she loves pizza, fish, and cheese. My goodness! Again!

I also noticed that some strange things started to happen. During this conversation, it just so happened we were listening to the same song without any communication between us! I began to feel as though I were being lifted off the ground. We began to send kisses, and I could sense feelings growing between us.

After a break, because Yulia had to take her dog out, we resumed the discussion by talking about movies, and we agreed on many things once again. I asked her what she thought about physical contact. This should be limited to kissing and sexual activities that are not overly clingy. The simple touch of a hand, a caress, or a hug are valuable gestures that should be put into action frequently. "Touch is important to me! I like even holding a partner's hand, hugging them. I do it as soon as possible, watching a movie, walking, anywhere!".

I had no words. Strengthened by such continuous confirmation, I decided to dare a little more. Since Yulia said she would like to have sex once a day, I asked her if she is a traditionalist in bed or if she is open to new experiences. She answered that she would like to have sex once a day with her beloved without any taboos. But, without that, she does not practice any sex.

"Excuse me for being forward. But absolutely no sex, not even self-eroticism?"

"Without love, I don't like sex."

Suddenly, we realized that we had been in front of our computers for almost four hours and that it was getting late. We left each other with kisses and a promise to talk again as soon as possible.

4 August

In the morning, I immediately logged on to the site and waited for Yulia. I couldn't wait to talk to her. I spent the previous day thinking about her and wondering what was happening to me. As soon as she logged on, I immediately told her what was going on. I was amazed to receive confirmation that the same thing was happening to her. We're experiencing the same sensations!

I tried to start a conversation and ask her what she would like to talk about. "You are the man, and you choose the topic." Wait a minute! Doubt flashed through my mind. Her availability might not be a trick to please me but an underlying weakness, total submissiveness toward the man. No, no. Or could it be?

I asked her how she slept the night before, considering I had not had a very peaceful sleep, and she replied: "In a short dress with a butterfly drawn on my breast." Evidently, she misunderstood my question. I replied that I really appreciate a breast like hers. I don't like breasts that are too small or too big. Yulia told me that she was a D size. Wow! I sent her a kiss on the breast, asking her permission first. "Yes! I like it."

Changing the subject, I asked if she could give massages, as they are something that I love very much. She told me that she knows how to do them and even took a course. However, because of her long nails, she can't do them. I expressed my disbelief to her. It isn't possible that we are so compatible, that we like each other so much. I asked her if she is telling me the truth because I feel like I am living a dream. She replied that dreams could come true. I am reminded of the movie *Three Steps Over Heaven.*

I decided to see what she thinks of my physical appearance and ask if she really likes me. She asked me if I still have a beard and a full-length photo. I sent her a photo of me without the beard. I don't have any recent full-length photos, so I promised to get it to her as soon as possible. When she received the photo of me without the beard, she replied: "You are much more handsome without the beard! I like your ears, eyes, lips, and chin!" I said: "I have a little bit of a belly, though I would like to get rid of it."

"The best way to eliminate the belly is to have sex! And I will help you!" I jumped in my chair.

"Yulia, if we were close, would you like to have sex with me?" "Yeeeeeeeeeeeeeeeee." I jumped up again in the chair.

Time passed, and at lunchtime, we exchanged photos of a gastronomic nature to imagine having lunch together. At least virtually. We continued to talk into the afternoon, and the conversation turned again to love, or how making love was the best way to express one's passion for one's partner.

It occurred to me to say to her: "Then it won't bother you if I tell you that I'd like to give you lots and lots of kisses on your feet, starting with your toes. Or that I'd like to kiss your belly or whisper sweet words in your ear. And I'd like to caress your head or be on a couch with you lying on top of me, your head on my belly while I caress you...."

"Continue."

"I would caress you all over. Your head, neck, belly, breasts, legs, thighs, and feet. I would cover you entirely in caresses and kisses. I would lick your ears and kiss your mouth, eyes, and hair. You are my woman. The only woman in the world! I got excited. Shall I continue?"

"Yes, yes, yes. I want to! And I'm turned on too."

"I would take your face in my hands and, looking into your eyes, say - you are my life, my light, love. Thank you for existing! - I would massage your neck. I would caress your back and breasts, hugging you all over and holding your body tightly against mine. Can you feel my excitement, my love?"

"Yeeeeeeeeeeeeeeeee. And can you feel mine? I would do all this with you if I could right now?"

"What would you do to me, Yulia?"

"I would start with a foot massage, massage the soles of your feet and all your fingers, then kiss your eyes, lips, ears. I would cover your chest and kiss your beautiful belly."

"Keep going. Don't stop."

"You will feel all my love, my passion, and sweetness. You are my man! I would caress you with my tongue, lips, eyelashes, breasts, whole body."

It began to grow late, and, to cool the mood, we changed the subject. I brought up the problem about meeting in real life, and I told her that I don't believe in long-distance love. And here is the first difference. Yulia answered that she does believe in it, and she asked me why I started talking to her. I told her I started talking to her, then something happened, and now I think I love her. The same thing happened to her, and now she loves me too.

#

We had spent practically the entire day together, and I was filled with love for this woman. I was about to go to work with my heart swollen with passion for Yulia.

Reviewing the conversations we had so far, I realized that I often talked about sex, even though I never made any explicit requests. Yulia had said she was not interested in virtual sex, as she intended to experience it only in the presence of love and in person. Perhaps this insistence of mine on sex could have been misunderstood. Maybe she thought I was a maniac. On the other hand, if she continued to answer my questions, there were two possible answers: either she was interested in me, or she was a maniac too!

My thoughts returned to the fact that she could be a scammer, a very submissive and weak person, or a nymphomaniac. I decidedly discarded that last thought and the idea that she was a weak person. From the answers I got, I could tell that she was not. She had her own ideas and convictions and knew what she wanted. The possibility remained that she was a scammer who was only interested in getting money out of me, but if so, she was spending a lot of time!

7 August

Over the last few days, there were some Internet issues, and we were not able to connect. Today I returned from work early, and magically everything seemed to be back to the way it was.

"Baby, it's been hard these days without you. I've been sad and thought about you a lot, but now that we can talk to each other, I'm the happiest man in the world."

"I've been sad too, and I'm so happy to be here with you again."

"Even though it's late, I'll stay here and talk to you as long as you want. I wish I could kiss you all over as long as my mouth has the strength to do so."

" Ohhhhhhh!! My sweet love. I'm happy."

"I can't sit in this chair. I have to do something. I want to hug you. I want to kiss you. I want to caress you. And I want to talk to you... I want you, Yulia, because I love you."

"Yeah! You say well. It's hard to sit because I want to hug you and kiss you too!"

#

I decided I absolutely had to see her, so I began to look into a possible trip to her place. The flight, the hotel, and everything else. Oh my God, what prices! I don't have much money, and frankly, I was hoping for a tax refund that would have helped me out. Unfortunately, the reimbursement was slow to arrive, so I began to figure out how I would make do with what I had. I started a systematic search for the lowest prices and managed to find cheaper solutions, but unfortunately, even they were still too high for my budget. I decided to postpone and see how the situation evolved.

13, 14, 15, 16, 17, 18, 19, 20 August

During the past several days, it was hard to get used to the idea of coming home and not being able to talk to Yulia due to her vacation. Something was happening inside me that I already understood but didn't think could happen at my age, especially not at such a distance.

I kept brooding over all that had happened, and the reality that she was a scammer was still possible, even if my heart was telling me not to believe it. I decided to verify if she was a known scammer on the Internet, but the result was negative. I was relieved. There was also another way to know for sure: wait. If she was a scammer, she would ask me for money with some excuse sooner or later. One day, while surfing the Internet, I came across a site specializing in seduction. Out of curiosity, I found myself looking around, and my attention fell on an article that explained how ineffective internet dating sites were. The author claimed that women who frequent these sites are preoccupied with work, kids, and whatnot; with no time for social relationships, they rely on these sites to contact men more easily. Hey! This is my situation, not Yulia's! He also said that it's easy to say many sweet words to each other virtually. But at the time of the real meeting, if there is no chemistry, then everything falls apart. It's true. And that's why I decided that our first meeting would be brief so that we wouldn't have to stay together for a long time if we didn't feel the same way. Of course, I wished it wouldn't happen, but my rational mind kept telling me:

"Be careful, never give up control!"

For two or three days, I sent her a text message with a few lines, just to keep in touch and confirm my love for her. She promptly replied. After three days, I decided to put her to the test. I didn't send any messages and waited for her to make the first move. My heart was in my throat because I was afraid she wouldn't write to me! However, her text arrived, filling my heart with joy.

21 August

Finally, the day of her return from vacation has arrived!

I couldn't wait to talk to her again, to exchange sweet words and experience those pleasant feelings that only love can give. Unfortunately, the Internet was still being difficult, and I couldn't communicate with Yulia. I sent her a text message to explain the situation, and we postponed our virtual meeting to another day.

At this point, I have abandoned all negative feelings about her, and I truly believe that she is interested in me and loves me. Therefore, I decided that the trip had to be done at any cost. But I had to find a solution to the economic problem, and so I began to study in detail how I could make this trip with what little money I have. The first thing to analyze was the duration of the trip. If I left early in the morning, taking advantage of the low flight prices at those times, I would have practically half a day with her. If I left late in the evening the next day, flight prices would still be low and I would have another day with her. In short, with just one night in a hotel and a low-cost flight, maybe I could make it.

Yeah, in a hotel. I didn't want to ask her to sleep over because it didn't feel right and, considering that we are actually two strangers, I thought it would be safer for both of us to be in a public place. This way we would have almost two days together, and it's more manageable in case there is no spark. We could consider ourselves friends, and maybe she could take me to visit her city.

Of course, if the meeting went well, two days would be

too few and we would want to spend more time together. However, we had to find an acceptable compromise, and the current plan seemed fine to me. We could always meet again another time, maybe for a week. All that remained was to find an affordable hotel. I couldn't wait to tell her that I had arranged everything!

24 August

I woke up early this morning to talk to Yulia and discuss the trip that would finally allow us to see each other and be together for some time.

"Baby, I managed to arrange it." I explained to her the choices I made regarding the duration and the hotel stay. Again she responded with: "You are the man. You decide."

No, that didn't work for me as an answer. I wanted to know what she thought.

"What do you think about the choice of the hotel, a public place for the safety of both?"

"As a first meeting, it's fine."

"Are you happy that we have two days at our disposal? This way we can also handle the meeting if it fails."

"I'm sure the meeting will be good, and two days is a good place to start."

Wow! I'm glad we agreed on the arrangements for this trip. However, there was something that didn't sit right with me. She was too cold. I didn't see any enthusiasm in her answers. Did something happen?

"Everything okay, Yulia?"

"Yes, Roger. Sorry if I'm a little weird, but I woke up this morning with a fever, and I think I got the flu."

#

It was done. There was no turning back. From that moment on, my mind was focused solely on that trip. All I could do was imagine what our meeting would be like. What kind of dress will she wear? How will she react to seeing me for the first time? I was dreaming about our first date. Everything had to go well, very well. I began to count the days until my departure.

29 August

Today is the big day.

I am happy because I am aware that, by booking my trip, my dream of meeting Yulia is coming true. Of course, a little fear always remains in my brain, as it is still a blind meeting. But the desire to meet this person, with whom I seem to have such chemistry, is now too great. Maybe I really found the right person. It is worth meeting Yulia and checking to see if she really is my soulmate.

With my heart pounding with excitement, I made the online purchase of tickets for the flight, departing on September 4, and for the night in the hotel in a room for two. I couldn't wait to get online and tell her that I had done everything and that soon our dream would come true. We would finally meet!

"Yulia, I have done everything. I booked the flight and the hotel."

"Great, I'll pick you up at the airport."

"I'm looking forward to meeting you, darling."

"Me too, Roger. I'll be waiting for you at the international flight gate."

"How exciting! I wonder how nice it will be to meet you."

"It will be beautiful, and we can finally be together."

#

As soon as I closed the chat, a terrible doubt came to me: how would I recognize her at the airport? It sounds stupid, but we hadn't thought about that problem at all. We should have at least told each other the type and color of clothes we would wear. No, we didn't have to. I would have recognized her in a crowd of thousands.

4 September

There it was, the last barrier between Yulia and me. The doors to international arrivals. The emotion was so strong. My heart was beating fast. My stomach was full of butterflies! The moment I dreamed of was about to come true. I would finally meet Yulia. I felt that everything would be fine, that she is the right person.

As soon as the doors opened, I found myself in a big, almost empty hall. At the end, a barrier separated the travelers from the people who came to greet them. Among them was Yulia! I glanced to the left side, where I saw a group of people, and among them, a woman in an elegant dress waving her hand. It was her!

As soon as I reached her, she kissed my lips, took my hand, and headed for the exit. "I love this!" A woman who can take the initiative and surprise her man from time to time is so adorable.

We made the bus ride to the hotel, sitting in the back row, hand in hand, almost without speaking to each other but staring into each other's eyes for long, endless moments. The heart doesn't want to know how to stay calm. The attraction and feelings I felt for this woman so far were only getting stronger.

The bus left us practically in front of the hotel. Unfortunately, the registration desk took issue with Yulia's documents, and they refused to accept us. Once again, Yulia surprised me.

"Come with me!" We left the hotel, and she headed to a

building not far away, which turned out to be some kind of police station.

"Wait for me here." She entered with a determined gaze. After a few minutes, she came out with the correct documents in her hand! I don't know what she did, but she solved the problem.

"Great, getting better and better!"

We went back to the hotel, and this time everything went smoothly. With the formalities completed, we made our way to our room. There. That was it. The moment had arrived!

In the elevator, we exchanged intense glances. We know that we were about to make our dream real. In a short while, we could give ourselves up to our passion, which we had held back for so long.

The meeting

It was five o'clock in the afternoon when we found ourselves entering our hotel room. As soon as the door was closed, we embraced and let ourselves go into a long, endless kiss. The desire to be together, know each other, and love each other was great.

To cool down the mood and allow us to fully enjoy the moment, I suggested we take a shower together. Finally, Yulia was there in front of me, and I could admire and enjoy her presence. All those moments spent dreaming of caressing, kissing, and touching her were now a reality. With every touch, a tremor went through my body. I could not believe it, yet it was true. My hands indulged in that craved body. From head to toe, everything was perfect. The hugs and kisses were so breathtakingly long. When I finished washing her gorgeous body, it was Yulia's turn. And it started again with kisses and hugs. I believe that the same sensations I had felt before were now hers. In short, the suggestion I posed to Yulia to cool the mood only made things worse. Being naked in the shower and washing each other warmed our souls even more.

When we got out of the shower, all we could do was let go and release our feelings.

And the night was pure passion for both of us. We were never satisfied with each other. The kisses, hugs, and loving effusions were never enough. We wanted to stay glued and to love each other without end.

I had never felt such strong passion for a woman, not even my first girlfriend when I was fifteen. Everything was perfect, and I felt complete harmony with Yulia. We were like Yin and Yang. Yes, she was the right woman.

Of course, I was lucky. I never thought I would find my soul mate through the Internet! But it worked. Finally, Yulia was here, next to me, and I was the happiest man on earth.

THE END

Made in the USA
Columbia, SC
18 November 2022

71658014R00020